The Adventures of AsparaGUS
Gus Discovers His Roots

Written by
Jan Ruehling

Presented by
Linda Rafferty

Strategic Book Publishing and Rights Co.

Strategic Book Publishing and Rights Co.
12620 FM 1960, Suite A4-507
Houston, TX 77065
www.sbpra.com

ISBN: 978-1-61897-266-8

Gus was hungry!

He knew that he was hungry because his little red dachshund tummy told him so. It rumbled and grumbled and tumbled, but it was not a happy hungry. His tummy did not sing like it once did when he was a puppy. Then, his little tail would wig and wag as fast as the pendulum on his grandmother Agusta's clock.

aaspara GUS

JANimals®

Gus trotted into the kitchen. "Oh, there you are!" Gus's mother, Agusta, smiled. "I was just about to whistle for you to come for lunch." Gus's mother always whistled for him instead of calling for him by name, as his friends' mothers would do. He liked that because it made him feel like he and his mom shared a special code.

As grumbly as his tummy felt, Gus nibbled at his food. He watched the pendulum of his grandmother's clock swing back and forth, back and forth, wig–wag–wig–wag. He studied the figures of the two dachshunds that stood atop the clock. They had been carved to look like Grandmother Agusta and Grandfather Gus. Their long tails were entwined to form the pendulum of the clock swinging back and forth, back and forth, wig–wag–wig–wag. Gus's mind was really on the green sticks with the curly tips that surrounded the face of the clock.

"Mom," Gus yelped, "what are those green sticks with the curly tips around the face of the clock?"

Gus's mother looked up at the clock and sighed. "Eat your food and don't ask so many questions."

aasparAGUSTA

5

"But, Mom," Gus persisted, "why can't you tell me what they are?"

"Asparagus, Gus!" his mother yapped. "They are called asparagus."

"But, what's . . .?"

"Gus, I do not want to hear another yip from you until you finish your food."

Gus stared at his mother, his brown eyes growing wide with surprise. Never had his mother barked at him like that!

Gus padded over to her and put his paws around her waist. "I'm sorry, Mom," Gus gulped, holding back tears.

"Oh, Gussie-poo," his mother whispered, using her pet name for him, "I'm the one who's sorry. I didn't mean to bark at you." Gus's mother gave him a big hug, and he hugged her too. "Let's sit down, and I'll tell you about your grandparents and asparagus."

"Many years ago," she began, "my mother and father—your grandmother, Agusta, and your grandfather, Gus—lived in a beautiful, green valley where I was born. Each day we would go to our asparagus garden. In the garden, we grew the same plants that are on the clock—asparagus. We were happy working in the garden and your grandmother would cook delicious dishes using the asparagus."

"Why don't we eat that kind of food now?" Gus asked. "We do not grow asparagus here." Before he could ask why, his mother went on.

"One day, we had to leave the valley. Mother and Father were very sad as they packed our belongings, which included a special box that held the asparagus seeds and crowns."

Wow! thought Gus. His mind filled with the kinds of crowns that kings and queens wear. "Were we rich? Did we live in a palace, Mother?"

Gus's mother looked at him and laughed. "No, Gus. We did not have jewels or money. Baby asparagus plants are called crowns. They are grown in gardens. Your grandmother and grandfather had a lot of patience, which they found was necessary to produce a beautiful, healthy crop."

Gus was disappointed, but he had learned something new about asparagus. He wanted to ask many more questions to learn even more and find out why they did not have an asparagus garden now. Before he could begin, his sister, Gusta, limped into the room.

aasaparaGUSTA

"Mama!" she cried. "I hurt my paw."

Gus's mother hurried over to her daughter. When Gus saw that his sister was not seriously hurt, he became impatient. More questions had just popped into his head. He wanted to know what happened to his grandfather and grandmother and why asparagus tasted so delicious.

Gus pranced back and forth, back and forth. He looked across the room at his mother and sister. *Gee,* he thought, *they look so much alike.* Each was long, slim, and golden. Each wore a white lacy cap. His mother's was old and worn, but she kept it starched and clean. His sister's was newer but always seemed to stay wrinkled and dirty. Now she was using it to wipe her eyes. Gus grinned. His mother would not like that! Gus knew that her cap meant something very special to her. While he watched his mother and sister, a plan formed in his mind. He would go in search of his own asparagus. His tummy agreed. It stopped rumbling and grumbling and tumbling and began to sing again! Gus darted out the door and leapt across the yard. When he spotted his friends in the distance, he paused with his right front paw raised in the air. "Goocille Ball" was fluffing the patch of fiery red feathers that

Goocille Ball

topped her white head. "Squirrley Temple" was licking her lollipop. "WaterMELONIE" was sunbathing, her seeds popping in all directions. They were down by the bay, waiting for their friend, the "Duke of Whalington," to swim up and play with them.

Draw your own

Duke of Whalington

WaterMELONIE

Gus watched his friends a little while longer. What adventures he would have to tell them next time he saw them! He whirled around and raced across the big field. He had asparagus to find! What a happy surprise it would be when he brought some home to his mother. Then she could cook the delicious dishes that his tummy was rumbling and grumbling and tumbling for!

"Aasparagus, aasparagus, aaspara, para, sparagus!" he sang as he ran. Gus ran and ran until his short legs became so tired that they would carry him no further. Panting heavily, he flopped down beside a stream. As Gus looked around, he realized that he was in a large forest. He began to sniff the air like dachshunds do when they find themselves in strange places.

So many new and unusual scents bombarded Gus's nose. The damp, earthy scent made him want to wallow and dig. The sweet, strong scent of flowers made him want to gather all the wonderful fragrances and carry them home to his mother. The sharp pine scent made him want to run and play with his friends. But there was one scent that stood out from all the rest.

It made Gus shiver and made the hair stand up along his neck. Although Gus had never smelled a scent like this before, he knew it meant danger.

The scent was not strong, which meant that the danger was not near. If the scent became stronger, Gus would still have time to quickly dig a hole in the damp ground and hide inside, because dachshunds' legs—although short—work like pistons and can dig deep and fast!

Staying alert, Gus lapped up a long, cool drink of water. He looked up and down the stream and decided to walk along the edge as far as the stream would take him.

As he walked, he thought, *Since asparagus grows in the garden, it must need a lot of water. So, if I follow this stream, maybe I'll find a garden full of asparagus!*

Gus splashed ahead. The cool water soothed his hot, tired paws. His big amber eyes searched for signs of hidden dangers as well as for signs of asparagus. The gentle breeze began to blow harder and the sunlight, which pierced through the tall, leafy trees, began to grow dim. The humming and buzzing and chirping of insects and birds began to fade.

Large drops of rain splashed Gus. He hated to get caught in the rain, but he had come too far to stop and find shelter. He shivered and jumped from the water as it began to rise.

Gus put his long nose to the ground. He ran and sniffed, ran and "Ooo-ooo-ooo-oooh!" Gus's nose skidded to a stop before his long body could catch up with it, and his face fell into a giant PAW PRINT! The same strange and scary scent that had bombarded his nose when he first came into the forest was now very strong.

The pouring rain made the ground muddy and slick. As Gus struggled to get up, his paws slid out from under him. He lost his balance and fell into the dark, angry, fast-moving water. The last sight Gus remembered before the rushing water closed over his head was a large, hairy mouth and sharp, white teeth grabbing for his neck.

Gus's nose woke up before the rest of him, and he felt it twitching. It twitched to a wonderful smell. Gus awakened and wriggled from beneath a toasty warm blanket. He stood up, slowly shook himself, and jumped down from the bed. His legs wobbled and his neck hurt, but he was not afraid.

Anyone who could cook something that smelled so good would not hurt me, anyone, or anything, thought Gus with a shiver, remembering the hairy mouth and the sharp teeth.

Suddenly, the door swung open. Bright sunshine filled the room. After the darkness of the storm and of the room, the sunlight hurt his eyes. Gus put his paws up to shade them. A huge shadow filled the doorway and gradually became a giant, hairy shape! Gus gawked as the shape turned into the largest cat he had ever seen! But there was something more. Gus had seen this cat before. But where?

Then he remembered! In his mother's bedroom on her dresser in a shiny silver frame, she kept a picture of his smiling Grandmother

Agusta, Grandfather Gus, and this cat! Imagine that! This cat was in a picture in Gus's own home! The final traces of Gus's fear vanished. He cocked his head to one side and watched the bright yellow cat with the orange stripes and the big green eyes. On his head was a tall, white hat with the letter "A" in the center of the wide band. The top of the hat was floppy and leaned to one side. He wore a blue apron with the words "a la Cat" across the front. But what the cat carried in his paw made Gus wiggle all over with excitement.

"Asparagus!" Gus yelped. "It really is asparagus!" Gus sat down on his haunches, threw back his head, and howled with happiness.

The cat dropped the asparagus, threw back his head, and roared with laughter. What a racket they made! A howling dog and a yowling cat!

When Gus heard the cat laughing, he stopped howling and ran over to the asparagus. He sniffed it and poked at it with his nose. He touched it with his paws. Then he spotted a stalk that was longer and greener than the others. He pounced on it and snatched it up with his teeth. Gus jumped back. He whipped his head around and let the asparagus fly. It flew across the room and landed on the bed. Gus jumped onto the bed, grabbed the asparagus, jumped back down, and ran over to the cat, still holding the asparagus in his mouth. Gus sat up as perfectly as any little dachshund had ever sat up before—his long back straight, his little red head erect, and his eyes shining like two new amber marbles.

The cat smiled down at Gus. "What a picture you make, leetle Gus, leetle AsparaGUS."

Gus stared up at the cat. "How do you know my name?" he asked in amazement as he dropped his asparagus.

"Because, mon petite ami, my leetle friend, I knew your grandpapa, Big Gus, and your grandmamma Agusta," the cat explained. "You look like your grandpapa."

"I have a little sister named Gusta, and my mom's name is Agusta. She was named after my grandmother," explained Gus.

"I do not know your sister, Gusta, but perhaps she looks like your grandmama, Agusta, just like you look like your grandpapa, Big Gus.

Gus continued to stare at the cat. His mind was all tangled up, but he stood his ground. "I do not understand. I just do not understand at all."

"Vienez! Come!" the cat said to Gus. "We shall pick up the asparagus, and I shall answer your questions as we eat our meal. You must be very hungry after all that has happened."

Gus picked up the asparagus, ran to the table, jumped onto the chair, and dropped the piece of asparagus onto the table. He could hardly wait to taste whatever it was that smelled so good.

Gus watched the cat carry the rest of the asparagus to the sink. His mind was filled with questions. How did the cat know his grandmother and grandfather? Where did the cat find the asparagus? What was the cat's name, and why did he speak in such an odd way? What was the other name that the cat called him? It sounded like asparagus, but it also sounded liked his own name, Gus.

Gus could keep quiet no longer. "Mr. Cat," Gus called, "is that your name on the front of your apron?"

"Oui, yes, leetle Gus," replied the cat. "My name is 'a la Cat.'

You may call me le Chat or just Cat. Mon mare et mon pare, my mama and papa, were French–Canadian chefs. They named me after their favorite way of preparing meals—one special dish at a time or 'a-la-carte.'"

"Thank you," replied Gus politely. "But why do you talk so funny? Sometimes I do not understand everything that you say."

"Ahhh," said le Chat, "I am French–Canadian too. Sometimes I forget and use French words when I speak. Then I must repeat my words in English so that you shall understand."

Gus munched on his piece of asparagus and thought about what le Chat told him. Finally, he asked, "Do you remember the other name you called me? It sounded like asparagus, but like my name, Gus, too."

"Mais oui, but, yes. I remember."

"Well," Gus continued, "was that a French word?"

"So full of questions, leetle Gus," smiled Cat. "Soon you shall be full of asparagus soup. "AsparaGUS full of asparagus!" Cat laughed. "Do you not see? AsparaGUS is not a French word. The last three letters of asparagus are the same as the three letters in your name. GUS. AsparaGUS! There you were, sitting up in front of me so proudly with the stalk of asparagus dangling from your mouth, looking like a smaller version of your grandpapa, Big Gus. I just put the two words together—Gus and asparagus—and called you AsparaGUS."

"I do understand, Cat, I really do understand! Gus is in asparaGUS! Gus is in asparaGUS! Gus is in asparaGUS!" Gus yelped and excitedly added in a second, "Asparagus will be in AsparaGUS."

Grinning, Cat placed a large pot of asparagus soup on the table. From it, he filled Gus's bowl and then his own.

"Is this your first taste of asparagus?" Cat asked Gus.

"No," Gus giggled, "this is." And he held up the stalk of asparagus on which he had been snacking. Cat laughed and laughed. Gus laughed and laughed. Happiness filled their tummies.

"I wish that my mother and sister could have eaten some of the soup too," Gus said, suddenly feeling homesick.

"Someday soon, perhaps they will," purred Cat as he walked to the door. "Follow me outside, leetle Gus. I shall show you my asparagus garden and tell you the story about your grandpapa, grandmamma, and their asparagus garden."

Gus bounced out the door. There before him lay row after row of what he had come to find—asparagus!

"It is so—so—GREEN!" Gus gasped. "Did you grow all of this asparagus by yourself?"

"Oui, yes, leetle Gus," Cat nodded proudly as he led the way over to a tall old tree that stood on the other side of the garden. There, he sat down and motioned for Gus to sit beside him.

Cat began his story by explaining that he had left his home in Canada as soon as he had been able to take care of himself. He had always dreamed of coming to America, had worked his way south doing odd jobs, and had always worked hard and honestly for his pay. He had stopped to rest in the woods beside the garden when he became tired of traveling. He had fallen asleep and was awakened by the sound of Big Gus and Agusta working in their garden. Cat had crept from his resting place and watched them while they worked. They pulled weeds, watered, and labored, but Cat saw satisfied looks on their faces. He had thought then that this garden had to be a very special place.

The more Cat had watched Big Gus and Agusta, the more he wanted to meet them, but he was very shy.

Early one evening, Cat was awakened from a cat nap by three pairs of dachshund eyes smiling down at him! Big Gus, Agusta, and their baby daughter had brought a picnic supper of delicious asparagus to share with him.

"Asparagus is what we are growing in our garden," Agusta had informed him.

Big Gus explained that they had been watching Cat all the while

Cat had been watching them! Agusta explained that the picnic supper had been her idea so that the four of them could become acquainted.

After they had talked, eaten, and talked some more, Big Gus and Agusta invited Cat to stay with them in the cottage, which they had built on a hill. That had made Cat very happy. In return, he promised to help with the garden as well as in the kitchen.

Cat told Gus that his grandparents had chosen this spot for their garden because of its rich soil, very much like the soil in the valley they had left behind. He explained that they had shown him how to dig trenches and to plant the asparagus shoots one foot apart.

"We watered the garden only in the evening," Cat continued, "and as soon as any weeds appeared, we pulled them up. We had the most beautiful garden in the world," Cat purred softly, with a far-away look in his eyes.

Because he did not say anything for a while, Gus began to squirm.

Finally, he said, "I think the garden is still beautiful. But please tell me what happened to my grandfather and grandmother."

At the sound of Gus's voice, Cat shook his head to clear his mind of its far-away thoughts. He scrubbed his paws over his face, took a deep breath, and went on with his story.

Cat told Gus that it had been raining for days, and the dark fist of the sky had dropped a net of gloom over Cat. Nevertheless, between downpours, he had carefully crossed the swollen stream and headed for town to do some errands.

As Cat had emerged from the forest, the black sky unclenched its fist and hurled handfuls of rain down upon him. As he huddled against the sudden drenching, he thought he'd heard Big Gus howling his name. "Caaaat, Caat! A la Cat! H–E–L–P! Help, Cat!"

"Whether it was the wail of the wind or the wail of Big Gus in distress, I did not know for sure," Cat explained to Gus. "I felt in my heart of hearts that your grandpapa, grandmamma, and their baby were in great danger and they needed my help."

"Where were they?" Gus yelped anxiously.

"In the garden," answered Cat gloomily. "They must have run out there when the rain slackened to save what asparagus they could."

He went on to describe how he had sloshed and slipped and slid his way back through the forest toward his friends. Not even the raging river that once had been a peaceful stream could stop him for long. He had clawed his way up a nearby tree and crawled onto a limb that had reached out across the flooded stream. Because the heavy rain had blurred his vision, Cat misjudged his leap to the limb of a tree on the other side of the stream. Instead of landing with all four paws firmly on the limb, he had been forced to grab a branch with his two front paws.

For a terrifying moment, Cat had hung suspended above the wild waters below! Carefully, he had swung his back paws upward until they, too, had clutched the branch.

Then, paw after paw, inch after inch, Cat had worked his way across the branch toward the limb. Once he had reached it, he flipped himself onto the limb and crawled down the tree as fast as he could.

Still fighting the pouring rain, Cat had burst upon Big Gus and Agusta as the rushing water was uprooting the small bush to which they had been clinging. Instantly, Cat had whipped his tail around a larger bush for support and grabbed Big Gus's tail just as Big Gus had grabbed Agusta.

"Hold on, mes amis, my friends. Hold on tight to each other," Cat had yowled.

He had begun to pull Big Gus and Agusta toward him when Agusta wailed to Cat, "My baby! You must save my baby!"

"Go! Go!" Big Gus had barked.

Cat had looked from his two friends, who had been struggling in the black, gushing waters, over to their helpless baby in her basket on the hill under the tree. A scary, sick feeling had washed over him as he realized what he had to do.

With tears in his eyes, he had to let go of Big Gus's tail as he had uncurled his own tail from the bush. Then he spun around and, streaking toward the baby, snatched up her basket in his teeth and then scrambled up the tree.

"This very tree that we are sitting under," Cat told Gus.

Gus had not taken his eyes off Cat since he had begun telling his story. Now Gus moved even closer. "What happened next?" Gus gasped, his eyes shining.

Cat continued. "Thunder boomed so loudly that it caused the tree to shake. Lightning tore open the sky, and even more rain poured through. Waves of water reached my tail and begun lapping at my back."

Faster and faster, higher and higher, Cat had climbed, still holding the baby's basket firmly in his mouth. Finally, they had reached a fork in the trunk of the tree where they would be safe and sheltered.

The baby had begun to whimper and tremble from fright. Cat had done the only thing that he had known to do; he cradled the baby in his big, furry arms to soothe and protect her.

After the terrible storm had passed, a rainbow with beautiful colors of red, orange, yellow, green, blue, and violet had arched its way across the sky. Cat had watched the rainbow appear, and hope had filled his heart that Big Gus and Agusta would be all right.

Eagerly, Cat had searched the ground below looking for some sign of his friends. Suddenly, he spotted something white dangling from a bush.

Holding the baby's basket firmly in his teeth, Cat had climbed back down the tree, placed the basket on the driest spot under the tree, and splashed across the garden toward the white object.

"What was it, Cat?" yapped Gus excitedly, jumping up. "Did you find Grandfather and Grandmother? Were they all right? What happened to the baby?"

Because so many questions tumbled from Gus so fast, Cat threw up both paws in a gesture of surrender, but the smile that crossed Cat's face did not erase the sad look in his eyes.

Gus noticed the sad look and stopped his wriggling and wagging. "Cat, you were going to tell me about the piece of white that you had found."

Cat's face now bore the saddest look that Gus ever saw. "I found the white, lacy cap that your grandmamma, Agusta, always wore," explained Cat. "I never found another trace of either her or your grandpapa, Gus.

"I like to believe," Cat continued, as he placed his paw around Gus's shoulder, "that your grandparents sailed away to plant another asparagus patch in another very special, peaceful place."

These two new friends—one, a little, young, spunky red dachshund and the other a big, old, fuzzy yellow cat—stared at one another for a long moment. The look that passed between them seemed to say, "We may be new friends, but we have discovered, just in the space of a spring afternoon, that we have something very special in common." Cat shook himself very hard to break the sad spell that his story cast over Gus and himself.

Gus did not forget about the baby that Cat rescued. There was something about her that puzzled him. He felt he should know her, but he had never heard this story before. Yet, something about her seemed very familiar, almost as if he had known her all of his life.

Oh, why are things so confusing! Gus thought as he stamped his paw in frustration. Maybe Cat could help him sort things out. "Did you keep the baby?" Gus asked hopefully.

Cat explained that because he did not think he could have cared properly for the baby, he had placed her in the care of a fine family, who had been kind to Cat when he had first stopped in the town.

Before Cat had said goodbye, he kissed the baby on her soft, golden cheek. She giggled because Cat's whiskers had tickled her face. Then, she reached up and nuzzled Cat's fuzzy cheek with her little nose.

Cat had swallowed back his tears as he had tucked Agusta's lacy white cap into her baby's basket. "You see," explained Cat, "I wanted the baby to have Agusta's cap because it had belonged to her mother."

The white, lacy cap! That was it! Suddenly, everything became clear to Gus. When he left home earlier in search of asparagus, he remembered his mother wearing her old, white, lacy cap that she treasured. The baby had a white, lacy cap. His mother had an old white, lacy cap. Gus now knew that the baby had grown up to become his mother!

Gus's face lit up like fireworks light up the sky on the Fourth of July! "My mother!" Gus barked. "My mother was that baby! Cat, you saved my mother's life too! Cat, you are a hero! A big, old, fuzzy hero!"

Gus's joy and excitement transformed him into a flying ball of fur. He hurled himself upward into Cat's arms with such force that Cat lost his balance and toppled over backwards.

Gus and Cat hit the ground together. Over and over they tumbled with Gus yapping, licking, and hugging Cat. Cat meowed, laughed, and tried to defend himself against Gus's overwhelming display of gratitude and happiness.

"C'est assez, leetle Gus, c'est assez!" Cat finally managed to gasp. "That's enough, that's enough!"

The two friends, both exhausted, now rested side by side. Cat lay on his back, his paws clasped beneath his head. Gus lay on his tummy, facing Cat.

"I knew that when I finished telling my story, leetle Gus, you would understand the relationship between your grandmamma Agusta, her baby, and you."

Gus nodded his head. "Yes, Cat, but it was the way you told the story that helped me figure out everything for myself."

Gus and Cat rested quietly, each content with his own thoughts. Suddenly, Gus spied another set of fresh paw prints near the asparagus garden. Curious, he scampered over to them. The prints were as large as the ones that Cat's paw made, but were somehow different. He placed his paw beside one of the prints. It was more than twice the size of Gus's paw, yet it had the same number of toes—four! The mysterious prints did not belong to Cat.

"Whose prints are these?" Gus called to Cat.

At the sound of Gus's voice, Cat, who had been catnapping, jumped up and ran over to where Gus stood. When Gus showed Cat the prints, Cat let out a frightening combination of hisses and growls. They sounded so menacing Gus cringed. Cat's eyes turned dark green with anger.

"The Phantom of the Asparagus Patch has struck again!" Cat snarled.

"The WHAT!?" Gus did not believe his ears.

"The Phantom," growled Cat. "Whoever or whatever it is strips my garden of the best asparagus plants." Cat showed Gus where asparagus plants had been ripped out of the ground.

"Do phantoms leave paw prints behind?" Gus wondered.

"This one does! I cannot catch him. No matter what I do, Monsieur le Fantome escapes me."

Cat prowled around the garden. He checked the ground for more paw prints and for more missing asparagus plants.

Gus could see that his friend was very upset. Gus wanted to stay and help him, but the sun was beginning to set. It bathed the garden in a golden glow. Gus had been away from home for most of the day, and his mother would be very worried that something had happened to him.

Gus made a decision. He ran over to Cat. "I must go home now, but I promise to hurry back another day and together we will capture the Phantom."

When Cat heard Gus's words, the frown on his face turned upside down and became a grin. "Oui, mon petite ami. Yes, my leetle friend," purred Cat. "Monsieur le Fantome shall be no match for AsparaGUS and a la Cat."

Cat held out his big yellow, fuzzy paw for Gus to shake. Gus shook it with both of his little paws. Then, Cat put his paws on Gus's shoulders and hugged him, first the right shoulder, then the left shoulder. Gus threw his paws around Cat's waist and hugged him back.

"May I please take a piece of asparagus with me?"

"Take your pick, AsparaGUS," Cat laughed, as he waved his paw from one end of the garden to the other.

Gus ran back and forth between the rows of asparagus. As he ran, he sang the song that he made up earlier in the day:

"Aasparagus, aasparagus, aaspara, para, sparagus.

Aasparagus, aasparagus, aaspara, para, sparagus.

Aasparagus, aasparagus, aaspara, para, sparagus."

Gus skidded to a stop. He found the perfect piece of asparagus— a long, slender stalk with a plump, purplish-green tip. Gus snapped it off from the bottom of the plant and tossed it high into the air all in one quick motion.

"Goodbye, Cat," Gus called. "See you soon."

Gus caught the piece of asparagus in his mouth before it could hit the ground. Then he spun around and dashed away across the stream and into the forest, headed for home.

Cat watched until Gus disappeared from sight. Then, Cat also dashed away, headed for the tool shed. He had to replace the asparagus that Monsieur le Fantome had stolen.

As he ran, he found himself singing:

"Aasparagus, aasparagus, I'll plant some more aasparagus.

Aasparagus, aasparagus, I'll cook some more aasparagus.

Aasparagus, aasparagus, I'll eat some more aasparagus."

THE END

(Or, as le Chat would say: "C'est Fini")

About the Author

**Author, Jan Ruehling and her sister
Linda Ruehling Rafferty December 2004**

Janet "Jan" Ruehling survived fifty-five years from spinal-bulbar polio. The disease left her completely paralyzed, including her lungs. To breathe, she used continuous mechanical ventilation. She was lovingly cared for at home by family, skilled nurses, and many friends.

In 1984, after the passing of her parents, she was determined to become self-supporting and started her Mississippi company JANimals. Although unable to use either her hands or her arms, she used her mind to create the "JANimals" characters and outline for the book some twenty-five years ago. Her line originally included wooden, hand-painted jewelry and T-shirts; they were popular sellers on the Mississippi Gulf Coast for many years.

Always thriving on challenges, she decided to complete the original children's book by dictating additional ideas and dialogues for this story to her friends, nurses, and relatives. Although this was slow going, AsparaGus was brought to life. "Gus" was based on her own miniature red dachshund who grabbed a fresh asparagus spear, which had dropped on the floor, and proudly pranced through the house with it.

Ms. Ruehling was born in Harrisburg, Pennsylvania. She moved with her family to Biloxi, Mississippi in 1962.

She survived Hurricanes Camille (1969) and Katrina (2005).

Jan appeared in numerous national, regional, and local television documentaries. Additionally, she had articles published in the print media. With around-the-clock care, Jan lived at home in Biloxi where she led an exceptionally active, productive, and fulfilling life. Jan passed away September 3, 2008.

- Linda Ruehling Rafferty (sister)

CPSIA information can be obtained
at www.ICGtesting.com
Printed in the USA
LVIW020918020912

296831LV00002B